Contents

Big Book of Aesop's Fables
ISBN : 978-93-5049-557-5

First Edition: 2013

© Shree Book Centre

Printed in India

Retold by
Sunita Pant Bansal

Published by

SHREE BOOK CENTRE
8, Kakad Industrial Estate, S. Keer Marg
Off L.J. Road, Matunga (W)
Mumbai - 400016 (India)
Tel : 91-22-24377516 / 24374559
Telefax: 91-22-24309183
E-mail: sales@shreebookcentre.com

The Cat And The Mice

Once, a big family of Mice lived in a large house. They used to have a great time.

The Mice ran around and played, especially in the kitchen and the storehouse.

A Cat also lived there. One day, he thought, 'This is my place and I shall not let the dirty Mice live here.'

The Cat began to eat them one by one. The scared Mice thought it was unsafe to go out of their holes.

The Cat wondered, why the Mice did not come out! So, he hung himself on a wall, acting as if he was dead!

The Mice came out of their holes and saw the Cat hanging from the wall. They cried, "You may try changing into a bag of

food. But, we will not come near you!" The Mice became more careful and saved themselves from the Cat.

Moral: *You should never easily trust anyone who has harmed you in the past.*

Glossary

Storehouse: a building for storing food

Dirty: not clean

Scared: afraid

Wondered: feel curious

Unsafe: not safe

Careful: being watchful in one's actions

The Fox And The Leopard

Once, a Fox and a Leopard were talking about their looks.

The Leopard was very proud of his shiny fur with beautiful spots. He always looked down on the Fox.

The Leopard said to the Fox, "You look very simple and ordinary. You are not handsome like me. Look at my spots!"

The Fox greatly admired his bushy tail, which had a white tip. But, he knew that he was not as good looking as the Leopard.

Seeing the Fox quiet, the Leopard got very angry with him. He wanted the Fox to agree that he was better looking!

But, the Fox was a wise animal. He said, "Your coat looks smart on the outside but I have a smarter brain

inside and that is the real beauty." Then, he walked off. The Leopard felt ashamed as that was the truth.

Moral: *An intelligent mind is better than a fine coat.*

Glossary

Proud: happy and pleased because of something one has

Fur: the hairy coat of an animal

Ugly: not pretty; unattractive

Bushy: very thick

Praise: to say good things about someone

Ashamed: feeling shame

The Fox And The Woodcutter

Once, a Woodcutter saw some hunters and their dogs chasing a Fox.

The Fox saw the Woodcutter and begged him, "Please show me a hiding place. I will be grateful to you."

The Woodcutter felt sorry for the Fox and showed him his own hut. The Fox hid himself in a corner.

The hunters soon came to the Woodcutter and asked him, "Did you see a Fox anywhere here?"

The Woodcutter did not speak, but pointed to his hut. But the hunters took no notice and soon left.

The Fox came out and started walking away. The Woodcutter yelled out at him, "Fox, you have not thanked me!"

The Fox replied, "I would have thanked you. But, somehow your thoughts and actions are not as kind as your words!"

Moral: *Real help means being true and honest to the person you are helping.*

Glossary

Woodcutter: a person who cuts wood

Hunter: one who chases and kills wild animals

Chasing: to follow something to capture or kill

Begged: to ask for something

Hut: a small house

Ungrateful: not thankful

He was happy as he did not have to fight on foot. He could now ride on his Horse and fight for his country.

But, after the war, the Soldier only fed his Horse dry grass and made him carry heavy burdens.

The Horse became very weak. After some months, the Soldier was called to fight in another war.

The Soldier got ready and placed the saddle on the Horse. But the Horse fell down as the Soldier tried to sit on him.

The Horse said, "You must now fight on foot, as you have turned me from a Horse to a Donkey!"

Moral: *Remember your friends in both the good times and the bad times.*

Glossary

Serving: performing duty

War: a state or period of fighting between countries or groups

Hay: grass that has been cut and dried to be used as food for animals

Corn: a tall plant that produces yellow grains

Burden: a heavy load that is difficult to carry

Saddle: a leather-covered seat that is put on the back of a horse

One day, the people saw that their city was in danger. The city was surrounded by the enemy.

The head of the city asked the people to give ideas to safeguard the city. Everybody gave different ideas.

A Bricklayer said, "We should use bricks to make thick walls to protect our city."

A Carpenter suggested, "We can use timber to make our boundary strong." Both the ideas failed.

At last a Currier said, "Sir, there is no material that is as strong as skin. Every man's skin is strong

enough to fight the enemy. We should stand together and fight for our city." All the men fought together and saved their city.

Moral: *No enemy can harm us if we are united.*

Glossary

Surrounded: to be on every side of somebody or something

Safeguard: to protect something or someone from being harmed

Timber: trees that are grown in order to produce wood

Boundary: something that shows where an area ends and another area begins

Leather: animal skin chemically treated to be used in making clothes, shoes, etc.

The Shepherd And The Dog

Once, a Shepherd in a village took his flock of Sheep to a hill for grazing.

The Shepherd also had a pet Dog, who did not let any Wolf come near the sheep. He was very ferocious.

Now, a Wolf wanted to eat the Sheep. He thought of a plan to trick the Dog and the Shepherd.

The Wolf decided to dress up like a Sheep so that he could fool the Dog and the Shepherd.

The next day, the Wolf wore a Sheep skin and joined the other Sheep. But the Dog recognised him.

The Dog told his master, "There is a Wolf among the Sheep. If you lock him up with them, he will eat them all."

The Shepherd was very happy with his Dog. He immediately found the Wolf and drove him away.

Moral: *A loyal and faithful servant is a blessing.*

Glossary

Shepherd: a person who takes care of sheep

Grazing: to eat grass or other plants growing in a field

Plan: a set of actions that have been thought of

Pen: an area, with a fence around it, in which farm animals are kept

Immediately: without any delay

Drove: to move away

The Dancing Monkeys

A King was very fond of dance and music. He had some Monkeys as pets.

The King got the Monkeys trained in dance. Monkeys are great mimics, so they quickly learnt the dance.

The Monkeys danced as beautifully as any of the courtiers. Everyone loved the performance of the Monkeys.

One day, a mischievous courtier thought of distracting the Monkeys during their performance.

So, when the Monkeys were dancing, he took out some nuts and threw them on the stage.

Suddenly, the Monkeys stopped dancing. They started running to gather as many nuts as they could.

They fought with each other for the nuts. Every one started laughing. The Monkeys never danced again.

Moral: *We cannot change anyone's basic nature.*

Glossary

Kingdom: a country ruled by a king or queen

Fond: having a liking for something

Courtier: a member of a royal court

Mimic: copy or imitate others

Audience: a group of people gathered to watch or listen to something

Distracting: to turn away someone's attention from something

The Fisherman And The Little Fish

Once, a Fisherman was fishing in the nearby river. He could not catch any fish.

Suddenly, he felt a small tug on his fishing hook. He pulled it out and saw a Little Fish.

The Little Fish cried, "O Fisherman! You are a nice man. Have pity on me and let me go!"

The Fisherman said, "I have been sitting here all day. I am tired and hungry. Why should I put you back?"

The Fish requested, "If you let me go now, I shall soon grow into a big fish. Then you can have a fine meal."

The Fisherman said, "Little Fish! I have caught you after a long day. I may not catch you the next time!"

The Fisherman put the Little Fish in his basket and went back home. Later, he had the fish for his supper.

Moral: *A little thing in hand is more valuable than a bigger thing in the future.*

Glossary

Fishing: the activity of catching fish

Fishing hook: a sharply curved device used for catching fish

Tug: to pull by making a short strong movement

Requested: to ask for something in a polite way

Supper: dinner

The Eagle And The Jackdaw

Once, an Eagle saw a lamb and grabbed him with his powerful claws.

A Jackdaw saw the Eagle capture the Lamb. He felt very jealous and tried to copy the Eagle.

He flew down to grab a large Sheep. But his claws became entangled in the Sheep's fleece.

The Shepherd saw the Jackdaw and caught him. He at once clipped his wings and took him home.

His children saw the Jackdaw with clipped feathers and asked, "What kind of a bird is it, Dad?"

The Shepherd replied, "He is a Jackdaw, but he would like you to think that he is an Eagle!"

The Jackdaw heard this and realised that copying the Eagle was not the right thing to do.

Moral: *When we imitate someone stronger, we prove that we are not only weak but stupid too.*

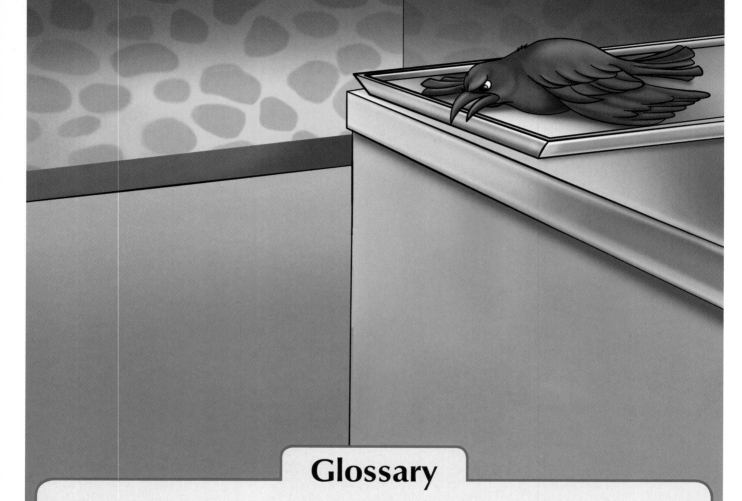

Glossary

Grabbed: to take or hold something suddenly

Claw: the sharp curved part on the toe of an animal

Entangled: to get caught in something

Fleece: the woolly coat of a sheep

Realised: to know

Clipped: cut

The apple tree did not bear any fruits. So, the Peasant decided to cut it down. He struck the trunk with his axe.

At once, a grasshopper and a sparrow, who lived on the apple tree, begged the Peasant not to cut the tree.

They pleaded, "Sir, please do not cut down this tree. The apple tree has given us shelter."

The Peasant ignored their requests. Suddenly, he found a beehive in a hollow in the tree.

As soon as the Peasant tasted the honey, he threw down his axe. He understood that the

apple tree was useful for many creatures. From then on, the Peasant took great care of the apple tree.

Moral: *Think not just about yourself but about others too.*

Glossary

Peasant: a poor farmer

Axe: a tool used for cutting down trees

Bear: carry

Pleaded: requested; begged

Beehive: a place where bees live

Chopping: cutting

The Bull And The Lion

A Lion living close to a village used to eat little children.

Soon, his wife, the Lioness gave birth to a Cub. When the Cub grew up a little, the Lion went out hunting.

He told his Cub not to leave the cave. But the naughty Cub got bored and went outside to play.

A Bull, who was passing by, saw the Cub playing all alone. The Bull killed him with his horns and was going to eat him when

he heard the Lion return. When the Lion saw his dead Cub, he cried aloud, "Who could have been so cruel?"

Please don't kill me!

A Wild-Boar, who had seen it all, told the Lion, "You have also killed many children. Their parents also must have wept like this!"

The Lion realised his mistake and since then stopped eating children from the village.

Moral: *You reap what you sow.*

Glossary

Cub: the young one of a lion

Bored: feeling impatient because you have nothing to do

Cruel: causing pain or suffering to others

Horns: bony growth on the heads of cattle

Mistake: a wrong action

The various animals took turns to perform. The Monkey danced from one branch to the other.

The animals liked his performance very much. They kept cheering him for a long time!

Now, the Camel was very jealous that everyone had praised the Monkey's dance so much.

He also wanted to be praised. So, he stood up and started moving about in a silly manner.

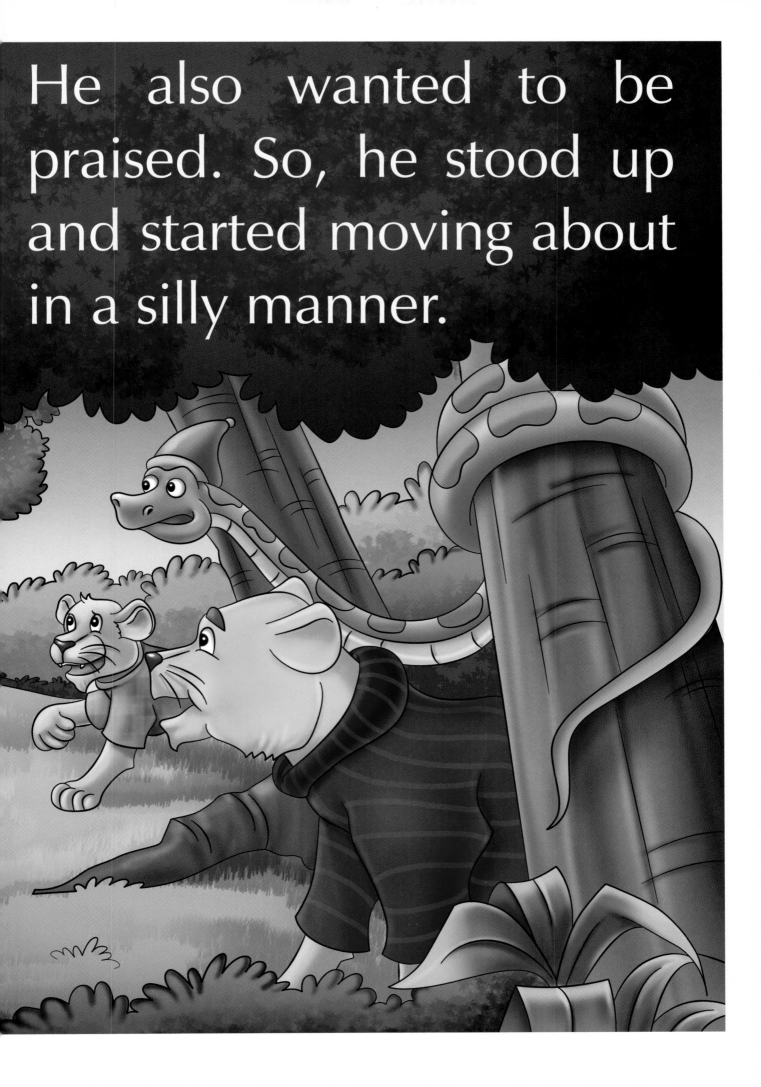

The animals did not like the dance as he neither twirled nor twisted. In a fit of fury, the animals

started beating him with clubs and drove him out of the gathering. The Camel learnt his lesson.

Moral: *It is silly to copy other people's acts just to be praised.*

Glossary

Entertainment: Something that amuses or pleases, especially a performance or show

Twirled: move around rapidly and repeatedly in a circle

Gathering: a meeting

Fury: violent anger

Clubs: heavy sticks, usually thicker at one end

Cheering: to shout with joy